The Erotic Way

The
Erotic Way

Diana Riverside

SIMON &
SCHUSTER
EDITIONS

For Laurence C. Park (you know who you are)

SIMON & SCHUSTER EDITIONS
Rockefeller Center
1230 Avenue of the Americas
New York, NY 10020

SIMON & SCHUSTER EDITIONS and colophon
are trademarks of Simon & Schuster Inc.

The Erotic Way is produced by becker&mayer!, Kirkland, WA.
www.beckermayer.com

From *The Erotic Way* packaged set, which includes a feather, a silken cord, massage oil, a velvet mask, a scented candle, and this book.

Cover design by Michelle Keller
Cover photography by Lisa Spindler/Graphistock
Interior design by Heidi Baughman
Simon & Schuster Editor: Janice Easton
Edited by Lissa Wolfendale
Thanks to Gillian Sowell

Manufactured in China

10 9 8 7 6 5 4 3 2 1

Library of Congress Cataloging-in-Publication Data
Riverside, Diana.
    The erotic way : everything you need from stories to playthings for
an amorous, unforgettable evening / Diana Riverside.
        p.   cm.
    1. Erotica—Miscellanea. 2. Sexual fantasies. 3. Erotic stories.
    4. Sexual excitement—Miscellanea. I. Title.
HQ21.R57   1999   98-17303
306.7—dc21   CIP

ISBN 0-684-84883-X

Contents

Foreplay

Enter the world of *The Erotic Way*—ten naughty scenes of passion and pleasure to compliment the elegant items of arousal included in this treasure chest.

The titillating toys in *The Erotic Way* collection are used in almost all of the stories as suggestions for some of the creative, fun, and freeing ways you can include these props in your own intimate activities. But remember not to let these steamy stories limit you—they're not intended to instruct you in your lovemaking. Rather, they're offered as a delightful way to stimulate, excite, and perhaps replenish your personal fantasy life, for the total satisfaction that every woman desires.

Of course while you are unlikely (and in a few cases, not advised!) to fully play out any fantasy in its entirety, it is possible that you'll decide you want to act out as much of a particular scene as you can. So if you and your lover are energetic and theatrically inclined, try dressing the parts, setting the room with suggestive touches, and saying the characters' lines using accents or changes in vocal pitch. Create new personae completely different from your own. This kind of role-play not only brings the fantasy to life, but also frees you to experiment with and expand your sexual repertoire, broadening your opportunities for ecstasy and complete fulfillment. (We've included some suggestions for inhabiting the characters' roles in the introductions to the stories.)

But if full-out dramatization is not your style, or if you prefer to read and use forbidden fantasies as a mental aphrodisiac to enhance sexual response and pleasure (as many people do), then do so! Read them through with your mate to plant the seed, then just fool around with the props and let your imaginations feed you!

Finally, remember that you don't have to share this delicious little volume with a partner in order to reap its benefits. Maybe one of you is shy and would prefer to keep its special brand of stimulation to yourself. Or perhaps you're currently between partners but still desire a way to nourish your own unique and divine sensuality. In any case, feel free to indulge yourself with private readings whenever you wish. Take this sexy little collection to bed and let it fill your head with lascivious scenarios that will sweeten your dreams.

Live and love *The Erotic Way.*

Headmaster

For this gothic fantasy of innocence corrupted, put away that contemporary black negligee or red satin teddy and rifle through your closet for the sweetest, most proper flannel nightgown instead. This is your chance to play the blushing virgin—an extraordinarily sexy role for both partners to experience, especially if in real life you have a high-powered job, fast-lane responsibilities, sophisticated tastes, or are just a bit "world weary."

9

$\mathcal{A}$s a young woman living in an austere 19th-century British boarding school, you are about to learn a most compelling lesson. On this particular night, high in the dormitory tower where you sleep, you have been awakened from a hideous nightmare: A gruff and surly thief stole in through the window, crept into your bed chamber, and towered over you, casting his chilly shadow across your languid body. Bending over you, he gently inserts a finger between your parted lips—so gently that you don't feel a thing. He lets the hot breath of your sleeping exhalations bathe his probing finger, the tip of your tongue just resting against his trespassing flesh. Suddenly, he seizes your lower lip between his thumb and forefinger and squeezes hard. At that moment, you wake, bathed in sweat and screaming. You decide to journey to the sitting room for a soothing read and rest.

Clad only in a high-necked nightgown, you pad down the polished stone steps toward the dark, carpeted sitting room, carrying a lighted candle in your trembling hand. Your bare feet are exquisitely sensitive to the surfaces beneath them and you feel a queer sort of restlessness in the pit of your stomach, as if a million tiny birds were taking flight. Suddenly, the light from your flickering candle is overshadowed by an imposing figure that seems to have risen from nowhere to fill the space at the

foot of the stairs. You gasp—are you still dreaming?—
and are about to turn and run when a familiar voice
hisses in the darkness: "Awake at this hour?"

It is the Headmaster—a man you have secretly
adored from afar yet found terrifying because of his
stern, commanding presence. But tonight his normally
booming voice is modulated to an intimate whisper and
it pours over you like honey. Your fear at being startled
is quickly replaced by those same giddy flapping wings.

"I'm sorry, sir. I couldn't sleep. I had an awful dream."

You expect him to chastise and perhaps even punish
you for being so weak and childish that you can't shake
off a silly dream. You quickly assure him that you tried—
you even wore this velvet sleep mask over your eyes to
blot out the moonlight—but you simply couldn't relax
enough to slip back into unconsciousness. To your surprise, he is not angry. In fact, he is sympathetic and tells
you that there are some tricks you might try to release all
that tension and fall into a blissful slumber.

"Tricks, sir? What tricks?"

All at once, he sweeps you into his arms and carries
you into the sitting room, displacing your nightgown as
he does, so that it rides above your knees, exposing the
pale curves of your thighs. You feel yourself go all hot
and flushed with shame, helpless. Desperately, you try to

wriggle the cloth back down around your ankles again, but it's no use—his giant hands have a firm grip on your torso, and thus on the uncooperative fabric of the gown. As he carries you into the drafty parlor, you feel a rush of cold air shoot up between your legs, but moments later he has placed you gingerly on the velvet settee and you are free to restore your gown and try to regain your dignity.

Using the flame from your candle, the Headmaster starts a fire in the hearth, then turns and pins you to your seat with his intense gaze.

"I don't usually give private instruction, you know. But I've been watching you lately and I've noticed what a very gifted student you are."

Watching you? This powerful, handsome man, who you assumed had no interest in the development of a young woman like yourself, has actually been watching you while you were unaware? There are those birds again.

"With a little tutoring, I think you could go quite far. In fact, that silken cord tying back your hair and that lovely sleep mask are the only tools I need to teach my secrets to such a precocious student. Shall we begin?"

"Oh yes, sir! I am your willing pupil!"

He sits down beside you, and with one hand begins slowly working the front of your nightgown up, up, up, as he trails his other hand along your shins, your calves, momentarily lingering at the sensitive spot behind your kneecaps, then lightly caressing the downy insides of your thighs. The fabric of your gown is now bunched around your hips, leaving you naked and exposed to the waist. Even though you press your knees together to counter your mounting shame, the triangle of hair at your pubis cannot be hidden. Then, with a tenderness you would never have expected, the Headmaster kneels at your feet and kisses the delicate bulge of your exposed belly.

"Lovely," he sighs.

Now he makes you shift around so he can pull up the back of your gown and expose your rear. As you sit back down on the settee, you can feel the slightly prickly quills of the deep red velvet rub against your thighs and vaginal lips. The Headmaster instructs you to rock slightly from side to side, and as you do, the velvet beneath your legs and buttocks shifts with you—a texture first sharp, then soft and smooth, sharp, then soft, sharp, soft. A little pool of wetness gathers between your legs, but it doesn't seem to quench the fire that burns there. This is all too much! You mustn't let the Headmaster see you thus exposed, and, before you know what you're doing, your hands fly to the hem of your gown, pulling at the bunched-up cloth in a futile attempt to recover your aching body and end this delightful, tor-turous game.

But the Headmaster grabs your wrist. The gesture seems harsh at first, and your eyes widen in terror to meet his.

"Please, sir, don't hurt me."

He softens when he sees your fear, and a slight smile flashes across his countenance. Assuring you that pain is the furthest thing from his mind, he reminds you that his only goal is to teach you ways of relaxation and release so that you can get some sleep.

His fingers ease their grip on your wrists and he begins to stroke your hands and forearms, kiss your tender palms, and gently lick and suck the tips of your fingers.

"The most important lesson is: Always obey your teacher. Of course, this is much easier to do when your willful, unruly tendencies are tamed. So if you can't con-trol those naughty, impulsive little hands, I have an effective solution."

He unfastens the silk cord wrapped around your ponytail, and your hair falls loosely about your face and neck. He grabs a handful of its redolent, luxurious thick-ness, and buries his face in it. He utters a deep, guttural sound and his eyes glaze over, but a moment later he checks himself and returns to the instruction at hand.

"First," he says, "we must remove all impediments to learning."

He whisks the nightgown over your head and tosses it aside, stripping you naked in the firelight. You feel the buds of your nipples shrink and harden under his examination, but rather than touch or taste them he only looks, making sure to draw out his pleasure ever so slowly.

"Now we'll teach your wayward hands to never again misbehave or try to hide your charms from the Headmaster," and as he says this, he ties your hands behind your back with the cord from your hair. This position thrusts your heavy breasts forward into his face and he can't resist; he allows himself one flick of his tongue on each aching tip before continuing. The sudden wetness of his mouth on your breasts, the shock of cold air when he pulls away—you've never felt anything like this before, and you moan slightly as your nipples begin to throb and pulsate.

"Finally, in order for you to commit these lessons to memory, I shall blindfold you with your sleep mask. With your sight thus restricted, you'll discover how the rest of your senses come alive."

Securely bound and blindfolded, your wet thighs spread open on the rough-yet-smooth velvet settee, your belly, breasts, neck, and ass completely uncovered and defenseless against the whims of your teacher, you are relieved of the need to protect your innocence. You are now ready to be an obedient student, eager only to learn your lessons and please your kind-but-demanding Headmaster.

Tomboy

Think guys are the only ones who like to play "catch"? Think again. That rec room closet filled with old sports paraphernalia can be a hotbed of erotic equipment. Try wearing nothing but his old high school helmet, shoulder pads, and cleats—you'll see your slugger choke up on his bat faster than you can say, "Strike!" Whether you and your beloved are full-time jocks or just weekend warriors, the variations on these games are endless. And if you consider yourself a sports widow, this could give you a new perspective on the great American "pass"-time.

$\mathcal{P}$ractice is over now and it's time for a long, hot shower and a rubdown. You bound across the field, sweaty and satiated, proud of your stellar performance out there. Lately you seem to be operating at optimum capability . . . could it have something to do with the new coach?

Man, is he hot—sort of young/middle-aged, with an irresistible combination of once-youthful brute strength and the refinement and seasoning of experience. And just because he's a few years older than those ridiculous baby-boy jocks who make up the competition, it doesn't mean he's lost his edge. He's still a tough, demanding bulldog, with his powerful running-back thighs; his cut, pumped-up forearms and biceps; and his perfect washboard stomach. That military crew-cut is beginning to turn a little gray, but those piercing, steel-blue eyes can still track a fly ball at 120 miles per hour, and when he fixes them on you, his aim is perfect.

Like right now. He's staring at you as you pass by the main supply room where he's straightening all the balls.

"Mathers."

"Yeah, coach?"

"Would you step in here for a moment? I want a word with you about your game."

This sounds ominous, and your heart begins to pound a hell of a lot harder than it does when you're in the middle of a high-stakes competition. But you know his brusque tone is only a way of keeping it professional, keeping the proper distance between coach and player. You know that underneath it all, he considers you one of his star athletes and a true asset to the world of women's sports. And you've seen the ravenous way he looks at your body when you're in the zone—lovely breasts bouncing up and down in a tiny sports bra; long, long legs encased in revealing spandex; tight ass held high, as you bound across the court or the field; silky wisps of hair flying wildly about, or else matted with moisture around a flushed face; tiny, buff waist straining as it lifts your rib cage and twists your exposed belly into the most extreme position (like a slave girl stretched upon the whipping post) whenever you're about to score. So maybe your heart is thumping for some other reason. . . . You step into the supply closet and try to control your heaving breath.

"What the hell were you doing out there today, Mathers?" he barks.

"What d'ya mean, Coach? I was at the top of my game! No one could touch me, I was like a well-oiled machine, scoring at every turn. I did you proud!"

"Yeah, well, you were scoring, all right. But I don't know if 'no one could touch you.' Looked to me like you were making contact with the entire team, getting 'touched' whenever possible. Just because we ran this practice session as a coed game doesn't mean you get to turn the event into a group grope. Team work is one thing, but you let those guys crawl all over you like you were some little hands-on cheerleader and they were the high-school varsity team. You're better than that and you know it, but you lack discipline. It's my job to whip you into shape, Mathers, so as part of your proper training, I want you to stay late today for a special coaching session. Just you and me, one-on-one. What do you say?"

"But I have to get to the ladies' locker room before the massage therapist leaves. I've got an awful charley horse, and she's the only one who can work it out."

"Forget her. I'll work on your damned charley horse—*after* we work on your . . . form."

His eyes caress your Olympian young body from head to toe. Then, burning with a challenge, they lock to yours. Adrenaline pumping, you return the look, prepared to show him what you've got, but suddenly you feel your usually aggressive, competitive energy implode under his lascivious gaze. It's like the two of you are engaged in a psycho-sensual game of arm wrestling, and even though you're strong, he's stronger. You are forced to give in.

"Okay, Coach," you purr, "I'll stay, if you want. After all, you're the boss."

His gun-metal eyes light up and you can hear his breath quicken ever so slightly.

"See? That's why you're a winner, Mathers. You have a winner's attitude."

He closes the door behind you, shutting you both up in the tiny supply closet surrounded by the bats, balls, and padded mats. The rich smells of wood, leather, and rubber mix with your natural animal scents, and within seconds, his hands are all over you, tearing off your work-out clothes until you are buck naked except for your gym socks and sneakers. Your lips lock together and you try to tear his clothing off, but he stops you, catching both of your wrists in his hands.

"See now, Mathers, you rely on the use of your hands and arms way too often in the important plays."

"Do I?"

"Yeah. Don't get me wrong. You *do* have a good arm," he whispers, slowly kissing one of your well-defined shoulders and then running his tongue along the downy-soft inside of your elbow.

"Mmm. A *great* arm, perhaps. And a great chest," more kisses, "and amazing abs, and, oh God. . . ."

He buries his nose in your ample bush and gnaws at your flesh with hungry teeth, never letting go of your wrists. He soon recovers, and suddenly you're standing nose-to-nose, as he faces you down with his eagle eyes.

"Nevertheless, if I've told you once, I've told you a thousand times: A woman's real strength is in her lower body." He takes both of your wrists in one hand and pulls them up over your head, using his other hand to stroke your long muscular thighs.

"See? Your real power lies in your quads, your hips, and your . . . hind quarters. Like a well-bred race horse." He slaps your derriere. "Giddy up."

You throw your head back like a mare in heat.

"Now what we need for this particular training drill is to find some way to restrain your hands," he continues, grabbing a bit of twisted cord, "so we can develop the source of your *true* female power."

Once your wrists are bound, he ties them to a strong iron hook fixed on the wall high above your head. This position stretches your naked body out to its full length—you can barely keep your sneaker soles flat on the floor—and you are about to complain when suddenly he pops a boxer's mouth guard in between your lips and makes you bite down hard. The thing fills your mouth like a gag, silencing your objections.

"I know that's not very comfortable, Mathers, but, hey, no pain, no gain."

Stepping a few feet back, he gently lobs a basketball toward you. You instinctively try to catch the pass, but when you realize your arms are completely out of commission you are forced to kick at it like you would a soccer ball. You field more balls with your legs, twisting torturously to bump them with your tender, fleshy buttocks; or you smash them back to him with a violent thrust from your rippled, exposed pelvis. Since you are unable to speak clearly through the gag, all that can be heard are the guttural grunts of your enormous effort, combined with the heavy breathing of your aroused opponent.

You do manage to catch the ball once between your knees and triumphantly refuse to drop or give it up no matter how hard he tries to steal it away. Just as he is about to quit, a gleaming drop of erotic dew falls from your swollen lips and lands like a liquid diamond on top of the rubber ball. He uses the stubby tip of his thick tongue to lap it up, then deposits it back in your pussy. You drop the ball.

Now he moves your sneaker-clad feet up onto his broad shoulders and bends your knees so that he can continue to suck, lick, and finger your hole. But just as you are about to come, he stops.

"Nnnnooo. . . ." you wail through teeth clenched around the bite plate.

"Discipline, my dear, hard work and discipline. You'll never build any muscle if you go all limp and squishy before we're done with the workout."

He transfers your lower body, bent knees and all, from his sturdy shoulders to an even sturdier stack of wrestling mats which he has pushed into place. Your upper body is still extended from the hook, but now you're squatting on the sticky rubber mat, feet wide apart, soles flat, heels tucked up against your buttocks so that your whole glistening vagina is open and exposed to view. It's an indecorous position, to be sure, but you're a fighter, ready to take and return whatever he dishes out.

"Ah, what a champion," he sighs, stopping to stroke your pussy hair and take your thick clit in his fingers, rolling it around like a marble until you moan. "With my coaching, you could be world-class. But not too fast. First you have to do me a solid."

He pulls out a brand new baseball mitt. The tan leather is as stiff and hard as a freshman. "You see this glove? Needs to be broken in, don't it? Oiled and rubbed, the leather moisturized and massaged, just like your ole charley horse. Think you can do that for me, tiger?"

You look from him to the mitt and back again and then nod your head vigorously.

"Oh, but listen to your silly old Coach," he chuckles, gazing up at your bound wrists suspended from the hook. "What was I thinking? You don't have a free hand, do you? Well, I'll tell you what. I'll just goop this baby up," squeezing a large dollop of massage oil into the mitt's palm, "and then you can work it *deep* into the leather with . . . your little ass."

He lifts your pelvis slightly and inserts the giant leather paw under your ass. Before you can even gasp, he has inserted the tip of the glove's finger into your rectum, then quickly forced your hips back down so that your rear door is opened by the thick protrusion of the glove and your cheeks are cupped in its well. As you sit, the puddle of oil within makes a rude squish. Slowly, steadily, you begin to make tiny rotations with your powerful *gluteus maximus*.

"Very good. You're going to make some young outfielder a very happy man—keep him from getting calluses. But why waste such effort on only one task when you are so multitalented? While you break in that mitt, would you mind softening up the grip of this new bat?"

He inserts the thick handle of a wooden baseball bat deep inside your vagina, gently pressing it past the swollen lips into the dark, wet cavity within.

"Stretching is an important part of any physical workout, true?"

And stretched you are. Your ass is filled, your sopping vagina is over-filled, your downy cheeks are both massaging and massaged. Everything is pressing and pushing urgently against your sensitive insides, filling and rotating, pumping, expanding, and engorging, until you are half out of your mind and ready to burst.

"Now, I promised you I'd massage your charley horse, didn't I? Hmm, let's see . . . is it in your neck?"

You moan and shake your head no, never stopping your pelvic gyrations in, on, and around the virgin equipment.

"Your calf?"

No.

"Oh never mind, you keep working, I'll just look for a place with a real tight, swollen knot."

He oils his rough fingers, and then, with a surprisingly light, sensuous touch, he rubs, kneads, and teases his way up your muscular legs until he reaches your stuffed, stretched genitals.

"Aha, I've found it!" he exclaims, gently tapping the erect and throbbing knob of your clit. "We'll have this nasty knot worked out in no time." As he massages your enlarged button, tugging at it, pressing and releasing it rhythmically, rolling it around in his masterful fingers, you continue pushing and rotating against the leather and wood phalluses until you shatter and explode like fireworks at the World Series.

Seduction Instruction

While some fantasies are best simply read on the page to plant a sexy suggestion, others, such as this one, beg for a full re-enactment. In the role of "tutor," you can indulge all your maternal instincts with the man-child you adore. Many woman are surprised to find how erotic these impulses can be . . . under the right conditions. And most men love playing the unschooled innocent boy—they get a chance to experience your nurturing side and take a break from always being responsible for initiating sex. But whatever your roles are, remember that this is just a starting point—there's no end to the exciting, sensual games you can play in a steamy shower, especially if you are a "creative educator!"

$\mathcal{T}$he rude beeps of your alarm awaken you early, and you moan out loud to no one in a feigned frustration with such a schedule. But a moment later you are grinning— you know you love the work you do. You *especially* love your dear little pupils—"your boys"—sent to you for tutelage by the Wentworth Academy. You would rise at *any* hour to ensure that these tender young things receive their daily lessons.

You head for the shower. The spray is at once fine and fierce; it teases and enlivens all your senses. Vigorously, you scrub off the last of the night's languor from your graceful, powerful frame, but when the serious cleansing is over, you indulge yourself for just a moment. Flipping the shower head from spray to pulse, you bend over and grab your ankles. The firm column of water beats against your swollen vaginal lips and streams wildly down between your legs.

Suddenly the doorbell rings. So early?! Lessons don't usually begin until nine! You step out of the shower, wrap your hair in a towel, and throw on a respectable robe. When you open the front door, you find Bobby. He's just another fine Wentworth specimen—a young man too shy and awkward to know how handsome he could be if only he'd stop caving in his chest to hide his embarrassment, or dangling his longish hair in front of his eyes to hide a sheepish grin.

"Bobby, what are you doing here at this hour? I thought our appointment was for nine!"

"I'm sorry, Ma'am. The Academy changed soccer practice to nine, so the only time I have for our session is . . . now. Oh, but, if you're not ready, I can come back another time! Except . . . not really, 'cause soccer practice and then . . . classes . . . and the only time I have is . . . now." His voice trails off.

"It's okay, Bobby. Come in. We'll work now and I'll finish my . . . ablutions . . . later."

"Your what?" Bobby snorts through his bangs.

"*Ablutions*—like cleaning, cleansing. Wait a minute, look it up!" you challenge.

Bobby opens his thesaurus.

"Here it is. *Ablution*: Cleaning, cleansing, purification, purging, catharsis . . . depuration?!"

"Like a *bath*, Bobby."

"Oh. But you look like you've already had a bath!"

"Yes, but—"

Your explanation is interrupted as Bobby begins to scratch his sunken chest and stomach through his shirt.

"What's the matter, Bobby. Didn't *you* have a bath today?"

"Uh . . . no."

"I see. And you expect to receive my services as a tutor—services that often require us to sit very close as we work together on some logarithm or equation—when you haven't even taken care to rub-a-dub-dub all those nasty, dirty little germs from your body?"

"Huh?"

"You know, you're not a child anymore, Bobby. You have all the . . . *secretions*—look it up—of a grown man. And good personal hygiene says more about a man than all the books he's read or the calculus he knows, or even the number of soccer goals he scored in his 'good old golden days.' Excellent personal hygiene is the most precious asset a man can have when he goes out into the big, bad, 'real' world, especially as far as women are concerned, *capeesh*?"

"Huh?"

"How would you rate *your* personal hygiene, Bobby?"

"I don't know. Okay, I guess. I mean I was *going* to shower, but I usually do it after soccer practice, and now they changed soccer practice to nine—"

"So I've heard."

"And the only time I have is . . ."

"Now." You wink. "Put down those books, young man. It's time for a lesson in Life 101."

He drops his books along with his jaw as you gently (but firmly) take him by the hand and guide him to the bathroom. It's still steamy from your shower, so you instruct Bobby to remove everything except his underwear in order to prevent his clothes from getting soggy and sticking to his skin.

"What? I can't do that in front of a *lady*—"

"Oh, don't be ridiculous. Don't think of me as a *lady*, think of me as a *teacher*—a devoted professional whose job it is to improve your knowledge of how to be a man, O.K.? You'd strip if I were a doctor, wouldn't you?"

"Yeah, but—"

"We're wasting precious learning time, young man."

He strips, as commanded. You are most pleased with what you see. His chest and belly, which appeared so skinny and concave when dressed, turn out to be trim, muscular, firm, and quite manly. His surprisingly broad shoulders taper down in a classic "V" shape to his narrow waist. Even narrower hips and a pair of *ridiculously* tight buns disappear into his baggy, boyish jockeys, which look like they could use a bath, too. His whole chest is smooth—without a hair in sight—but his torso is lavishly striated with washboard muscles from groin to gullet, covered by skin so tender it's like a baby's behind.

He's probably received his share of wet towel lashings in the locker room to redden and toughen up that velvety skin, and you think of what you'd give to be a fly on the wall to witness that.

You direct him to sit on the toilet. His eyes register panic, but you just chuckle.

"I don't mean *that!* I just mean sit on *top* of the toilet with the top *down*, like a chair, so you'll be comfortable while you observe. But here's your first lesson of the day: A gentleman should *always* put the seat *and* the top down when he's done. You never know when or where you'll be ordered to sit and you wouldn't want to fall in, would you?"

Obediently, he closes the lid of the toilet bowl and sits. (It never hurts to train a young man in *all* the ways to please a woman!)

"So. One way *some* people try to get around maintaining adequate personal hygiene is to wear perfumes, deodorants, or other such products as a mask. This is unacceptable, for there is no point in 'gilding the lily' if the lily smells like skunk weed, is there? I, however, have already taken a shower—as you have so keenly observed—so now it is the proper time for *me* to be anointed with after-bath products."

You hand him a container of silky talcum powder

and a long feather for its application. Standing directly in front of him, you place one foot on the edge of the toilet seat, right between his knees, and let the sides of your robe fall away from your long, shapely leg. You guide his hand, teaching him to use the feather with great finesse as he dusts you with the soft, scented powder, working from the backs of your knees to the soles of your feet, one leg at a time.

"See how you're barely grazing me with the feather, Bobby? That's how light a man's caress should be when he first touches a woman. Not that I'm a woman, of course, I'm just your instructor, but, oh my, you are a *very* gifted student. You catch on right away." Now it's your turn to trail off in a low moan.

You daintily open your robe a bit more and contract your pelvis, thrusting your still damp, sweet bush up and forward, right into the face of your willing student. Wordlessly, you show him how to use the feather's downy end to tickle the sensitive tip of your clit. As it swells, the tiny pink mountain begins to peek out from between your labia. Filling, stiffening, pulsating, this oasis of pleasure seems to reach and grasp like a tiny fist, begging for satisfaction. . . .

You open your robe completely and let it drop, exposing your lavish womanly body to this neophyte's view. He yelps—the dear little puppy dog—as you squirt scented massage oil into his hands and draw them to your shoulders, letting him know that now he must moisturize and massage your delicate skin. He eagerly attacks the assignment, but you have to gently remind him to pay *some* attention to your arms, belly, neck, and back instead of focusing so completely on your (to use *his* words) "awesome breasts!" He simply can't help himself; he cups and cuddles the full, round treasures as if fondling them were a matter of life or death. Indeed, if you didn't know he was all grown up, you'd think they *were* his only source of sustenance. This baby boy acts like he still needs his mommy, so intense is his suckling of your dark, firm nipples.

You can tell that any minute now, he is going to soil those already questionable underpants.

"Okay, my little protégé, into the shower with you," you command. He looks like he's going to pass out; his eyes are wild and pleading, his sheepish grin is twisted into an expression of erotic longing, but he's still able to perform the tasks you assign him in order to complete his education. Tearing off his shorts, he leaps into the pounding hot shower and awaits further instruction.

"Bend over."

You lather your long, strong fingers with the bar of

soap, then slip your middle finger up his ass, making sure the smooth hole gets a good, long cleansing, in and out, in and out.

"We must get to all the hard-to-reach places," you say.

"Ohhhh, ahhhh, pleeeeeeeze!!!!" he cries with pleasure. You know he needs to come, but . . .

"Wait!" you warn him. "One last lesson in 'personal hygiene.'"

With your finger still inside his rectum, you kneel on the bath mat in front of the shower, bringing your face right up to the young stud's erect, virgin cock.

"Super-sensitive areas should really receive a tongue bath," you inform him. Then you go to work.

Private Business

This workplace scenario flirts with the eroticism of power, domination, subservience, and humiliation, and conjures the intimate connection between pain and pleasure. No matter what kind of job you actually have—whether you are a high-stakes career woman like the heroine of our tale or a full-time wife and mother—you still have to deal with the same pressures, gender expectations, and sex-charged dynamics between men and women as everyone else in today's competitive world. So use this scene to explore your own impulses to control, "be on top," or demand satisfaction—if not in your daily grind, at least in your nightly one! (By the way, this is not just to please you; he may go nuts for the chance to be passive, especially if he has a demanding, aggressive job.)

$\mathcal{Y}$ou are the wildly successful head of a major multinational corporation. Most of the people who work under you are young, ambitious men eager to do your bidding. As powerful as you are, they don't realize what lurks behind your serious, button-down dress and manner—they see you only as The Boss, almost genderless. But underneath your severe exterior is an ultra-feminine, satin-and-lace goddess with all the needs of a woman, only you're a woman who can be even more severe when crossed by an overly ambitious male.

Take Jenkins, in accounting. He may look like a young buck, but rumor has it he is bucking for your position! Such insubordination cannot be tolerated in business. Perhaps, you think, it's time to take a break from making deals and turn your attention to correcting the behavior of your upstart employee. You buzz your secretary.

"Send in Jenkins."

When he enters your inner sanctum—plush carpet, gigantic desk, oversized windows—his usually confident good-looks turn lanky and awkward. What a deliciously cruel twist to see this young and cunning cricket suddenly pinned to the board, for an intimate examination by the resplendent butterfly. You pick up his file.

"Mr. . . . ?"

"Jenkins, ma'am."

"Ah, yes."

You pause to look directly at him and see his eyes of fire. You hadn't noticed that before, but now you are being scorched by them.

"Was there something you wanted, ma'am?" he stutters. "Otherwise, I really must get back to my desk. I left several rows of figures untallied."

Weasel. "You seem very dedicated to your work, young man. But I wonder. Are you *really* dedicated? Or just *ambitious*? Sit down, Joke-ins."

Seated, he shrinks from the volley of your own eye-fire, and he looks smaller, meeker, more shriveled. You sit tall in your huge leather executive chair, and, coolly crossing your legs, begin to swivel ever so slightly back and forth. Only the repetitive squeak of the chair breaks the silence, as it responds to each of your tiny, insistent, pelvic gyrations.

"I understand that you think that *you* should be running things around here."

He starts to sweat.

"Tell me, Jinx-skins," you continue, "why do you think I'm the head of this organization?"

"Well, um, because you're as good at making money as any of the guys on The Street?"

"Actually, I'm better. But then I'm not one of 'the guys,' am I, Jankoff?"

You stretch one leg out on the desk and gently kick off your black stiletto pump—the only deviation from your otherwise conservative attire. It flies across the room and lands in his lap, but not before the sharp heel scratches a tiny wound onto the back of his hand. You smile when you see the slim red gash—you've drawn blood! He sucks the wound with his pale lips and stares at you, aghast, but after a moment he can't resist lifting the shoe to his face and inhaling deeply, savoring the musky aroma wafting from the inner sole.

He moans, sinking deeper into his chair, and his entire body goes limp except for the growing bulge in his pants. That nasty serpent seems to grow and grow until it is like a thick divining rod pulling him violently toward you—the Boss, the Commander—but his erection has forced his baggy trousers into a crotch-tent and impairs his movement.

"Jaglom, bring me my shoe."

He can't move.

"I said, bring me my shoe, this minute, or you'll be wearing it rather than sniffing it like the bad, bad dog you are."

He tries desperately to stand, but his normally rippled muscles are reduced to quivering jelly and his swollen penis is a thick weight around his hips, pulling him forward and off balance. He drops to his knees and moans again, looking to you in a wordless plea for forgiveness.

"That's all right, Jerky. You can crawl. Now bring me my shoe and put it on my foot!"

He quickly shuffles across the carpet to the side of your desk, panting and holding your precious shoe in front of his face like a mongrel with a coveted bone.

"Feel my silk stockings, Junkbonds," you purr. "The 'guys on The Street' don't wear these now, do they? Or these. . . ."

You slowly pull your demure knee-length skirt up, up and up, until you expose the black satin garters adorning your feminine thighs.

"Or *this.* . . ."

You hike the skirt up even further to reveal a lacy garter belt slung low, encircling your restless hips and pulling taut against your round, firm belly. And what a surprise—despite the other provocative bits of lingerie, you're wearing no panties at all!

Jenkins lets loose a sound that goes far beyond a moan. It's a deep, wounded sound—a cry for help, a beg for mercy—that offers up every bit of his useless little soul to you. You stare down at the sniveling lump crouched at your feet.

"Tell me you never wondered—you and all my other little worker bees—what the big, bad Boss-lady wore under her drab business suit. Tell me you never gossiped among yourselves, making childish, schoolboy bets that she wore a jock strap, or perhaps an iron chastity belt. Tell me, little man!"

"No! I mean, yes! I mean, we did wonder, Madame, but, but, we could never imagine *this*. It's so—*you're* so—so beautiful!"

Look at that. First you draw blood, now tears. This *is* a productive meeting.

"Stop leaking, Jughead, it's unprofessional. And take that 'thing' out of your pants."

Jenkins suddenly regains his energy and rushes to comply. His cock is stupendous—longer and thicker, more purple with passion than you had imagined—and for just a moment, you lose your bearings. Your lips purse slightly and you feel your ample juices begin to ooze out onto the leather chair. Luckily the sight of him rising unprotected from his otherwise fully clothed body is too comically absurd; you easily recover your poise in order to further the game.

"If you think you're so ready to run the company,

Jiggers, let's test your problem-solving skills, shall we?"

Slowly, seductively, you again slip off your high-heeled pump, and, holding it by its long, pointed stiletto, twirl it in front of his face.

"I'm tired of wearing this shoe, but wherever can I put it? There's not a shoe rack in sight."

Without skipping a beat, Jenkins forces his hips forward to offer his swollen knob for your personal use.

"Ah, what a creative solution," you whisper, delicately dropping the shoe onto his thrust-up dick, where it hangs suspended in front of him. Next you use your shod foot to lightly kick him into the space under your desk. Crouched over between your legs, peering obediently up into your cold face, he is truly a faithful hound.

Reaching inside your blouse, you undo your bra, pull it out like a magic trick, and dangle it in front of his glassy-eyed face. To his surprise, it's not really a brassiere at all, but more of a thin velvet mask that ties in the back—barely big enough to cover much more than your swollen nipples—and right now it's completely limp from the warmth of your body.

"Look, Jesters, now you can tell your friends they were all wrong about the old-maid corset they were sure I wore. This Boss-Lady wears nothing but a tiny blindfold across her chest to keep her naughty worker bees from glimpsing even a *hint* of her erect nipples. Other than that," you murmur, as you slowly caress your breasts through the thin layer of your blouse, "her glorious, ample bosom is entirely free."

You cup the soft, firm globes in your hands and shake them playfully like they were bouncing baby twins. "Every time The Boss laughs with glee at the closing of a deal or the doubling of an asset, her beautiful tits bounce and jiggle wildly, unimpeded, under her stiff, somber jacket. You go back to the typing pool and tell them that."

Another tear slides out of Jenkins' eye. Using a corner of the velvet brassiere, still full of your scent, you mop it up. Then you tie the nipple cloth around his eyes, cruelly blinding him. Next, you pull a silken cord from your desktop drawer (a standard office supply in all proper executive suites) and bind his hands behind his back. Finally, the *pièce de résistance*: a tiny squeeze bottle of massage oil which you stick in his mouth like a plug, forcing his lips into a round, subservient "O." The little red nub on the bottle's spout sticks out like an aroused clitoris poking through its puffy hood; and the whole get-up reduces your employee to a lewd joke.

You begin once more to swivel in your chair, again making tiny arcs back and forth, back and forth. As before, the chair responds with a slew of squeaks and squeals.

"Now, let's find out if you can be of any real use to this organization."

With the heel of your shod foot you force his head and shoulders down and into the seat of the chair.

"Get to work, Janitor!" you say. "Find that squeak, figure out where something is *rubbing* up against something else, lubricate it, and make it smooooooth. And you better not let my precious shoe drop or you'll find yourself officially down-sized!"

Blindly, desperately, he bites down on the bottle and ejaculates streams of scented oil from between his lips, but of course to no avail! Instead of lubricating the mechanical squeak, your private parts receive a slick oil bath. While you inwardly revel in the sensation, you still continue to show him who's boss.

"Do it, Jackoff, fix it!"

More oil, more squeaking.

"My God, you are incompetent," you growl, pressing your heel into his flesh. "You can't even do the job of a low-level handyman. What makes you think you could run a *company*?!"

Like a mad hound, he thrashes about trying to pin-point the problem, all the while keeping your high-heeled shoe balanced on his erection, but the irksome chair continues to squeak.

"Forget it, Jimbo. You're fired."

He whimpers from beneath your desk, but you are less than sympathetic.

"It's no good arguing with me, I've made an executive decision. You disgust me."

Suddenly his puppy dog eyes regain some of their fire underneath the mask and he sits back on his heels. He spits out the bottle, then dives, tongue first, into your well-oiled slit. Lapping, sucking, gnawing, licking, he labors happily at this inner-office assignment, just like a good worker bee should, until you moan, heave, shake, and ultimately beg *him* for mercy.

Shopping Secrets

Some say the life of a stay-at-home housewife is tedious and unfulfilling—but you disagree. In fact, your home-making career includes a colorful variety of tasks, responsibilities, and challenges, unlike so many dull jobs out there in the workplace. Plus, when you work a nine-to-five gig, you have to take care of your personal chores on a crowded Saturday along with all the other working stiffs. Nope, not for you. You like having the flexibility to, say, shop, any time at all. And, as you are about to prove on today's spree, this particular perk places the job of homemaker at a surprisingly high level on the scale of "worker satisfaction"...

$\mathcal{A}$h, shopping . . . one of life's great pleasures, one of society's sweetest gifts. To roam through rack-forests hung with glamour and high drama, to sort through mountains of nothing less than wearable art, until you find "just the thing"—perhaps a quintessential strappy little black number with a deliciously scandalous hem?—shopping is truly the sport of the Gods. And with your flexible schedule you can indulge in the sport anytime you like. On this particular Tuesday, you show yourself to be quite an Olympian.

With a superb combination of grace and alacrity, you wend your way through the giant pleasure palace of the local department store, buying here, buying there, buying buying everywhere. China, linens, bathware, fragrances. A naughty little side trip to the shoe department for a quick *tête á tête* with a pair of polished leather spike-heeled sandals from Florence around which you could start a major religion. A low-fat lunch in the *Grotto d'Yogurt Frieze*, and then back to the sacred arena to do glorious battle with the lions of fashion. The final event? Lingerie.

As you enter the "Intimates" department, you notice that the lighting changes; instead of standard industrial florescents, the place is lit by soft incandescent bulbs which flatter the skin and make the rows and rows of flesh-colored silk and satin panties, hanging like forbidden fruit from their displays, simply glow. The air is perfumed, the piped-in music is romantic and slightly suggestive. You love this section of the store—it's like an oasis in the middle of a stormy consumer's sea—and the merchandise seems to sing a siren's song full of mystery, allure, and feminine secrets.

But when you look around for your favorite salesgirl, Monique, she is nowhere to be found. How can this be? The whole shopping experience just won't be the same without the petite French brunette with the heavy-lidded eyes. What will you do without her soft, delicate hands gently fitting your voluptuous flesh into a strapless bra or a tight, glossy "body shaper"?

But the only salesperson on the floor seems to be that young man standing behind the counter. A man in lingerie? That's odd. Although you have to admit, his shell-shocked expression does make you smile. Why, he's embarrassed, the poor baby! Maybe you can help each other. . . .

Ducking behind a rack of Shape 'n Firm foundation garments, you slip off your running shoes and step into your new, drop-dead Italian heels. They add a sleek couple of inches to your already impressive frame, and the kid-glove feel of the leather straps, like tight slave bracelets around your insteps and ankles, changes your gait from a galloping shopping stride to a sultry slink.

You slink right on up to the terrified salesman, your little sacrificial lamb. He's wearing one of those pathetic white paper carnations that indicate he's a store official, and a little plastic name tag that reads "Victor."

"Excuse me, Victor. Is Monique here?"

"Um, no ma'am, I'm sorry, she's not. I'm afraid I'm the only one working this department today. But if you come back tomorrow, I'm sure she'll be available then."

"That's okay," you purr, "I'm sure you'll do just fine."

His face flinches slightly. Oh, why did they have to assign him *here*, of all places?! Just because he's a rookie and the low man on the totem pole, was it really fair to make him work lingerie the *one* day that French tickler had to call in sick? Most of his morning has been spent alternating between quelling his embarrassed blushes and squelching his raging erection. There isn't a half-slip or panty, a bra cup or nightie that he hasn't imagined fondling—perhaps inhaling the scent of perfumed lace, or slowly dragging the fabric across and around, over and under his throbbing dick. When he isn't thinking about pleasuring himself in the piles of feminine silks and satins, he imagines each and every one of the thousands of ladies' underwear items filled with the curvaceous, warm, redolent body of a real, live woman. He pictures them surrounding him in this forsaken place—redheads and blondes; striking women of color and women pale as pink ice; old, young, short, tall, round and luscious or slim and sylph-like. A whole harem—all clad in nothing but these delicate little wisps of silk hanging on their tiny hangers that for the moment only suggest the shape of the real thing. And now, he trembles, here is an actual woman from his fantasies, leaning so far across the counter that he can feel her hot breath on his face.

"Well? Are you going to help me?" you ask.

His tongue seems to have a life of its own and thickens with fear and longing. It wants to taste your lips and tongue, to trace the outlines of your eyelids, your swan neck, the rosebuds of your delicate nipples . . . but instead, it is forced to answer, "Yes. Yes, of course."

"Good. I'm looking for several items. Panties, size 6; a low-cut brassiere, 34D; silk stockings, extra-long; oh, a garter belt, of course, and . . . hmm, I don't know . . . I was wondering . . . what about a corset?" You take his hands and gently place them around your tiny waist. "Do you think I need one?"

"N-n-no ma'am," he squeaks.

"Well, better bring me one to try, just in case. I'll be

in dressing room three." You turn on your Florentine heels and start to saunter away.

"Wait, ma'am! I don't know which—what—style. . . . " His faltering voice trails off as he meekly gestures toward the huge array of merchandise which surrounds him and tortures his very being.

"Oh, you look pretty familiar with the stock. Why don't you just pick out . . . your favorites?" You wink, then slide back to the dressing rooms.

❧

A few minutes later there is a knock on your dressing room door. You peer over the top of the door and see your poor salesman standing just outside in the corridor. His back is toward you as he faces shyly away, and his posture looks like he's ready to bolt, but there is one bold arm holding out an array of lacy lingerie as a sacred offering, and you notice that it's the sexiest in the store.

"Ooh, Victor, good taste. Black lace, just what I like."

His head is still turned. "Great. Then I'll just be going—"

"—At least I *think* I like it," you interrupt, "but how can I tell when they're all floppy and flaccid like that in your hands? They must be tried on."

He tries to hand the garments to you without moving, but his arm simply won't stretch and grow at the same rate as his penis. He invites you to come get the goods.

"No, silly," you counter, "I can't come out there, I'm all naked. . . ." You're sure you just heard him groan. Or was that a whimper? "Come on, Vic, why don't you bring those goodies in here to me yourself, O.K.?"

He hesitates. You poke your head outside and plead.

"After all, that's what Monique does," you say, "She fetches whatever I desire. Then she brings it right into my dressing room and locks the door behind her so no one can discover us in our little den. She's a very 'hands on' salesperson. She hooks the hooks and tightens the laces and makes sure everything works just right. Sometimes she bends me over and guides my jiggling, unruly breasts into the bra cups, smoothing the satin across the mounds, making sure the nipples fit just so into the tiny indented tips of the cups . . . don't you want to give me personal service, just like Monique?"

Finally, he finds his tongue, if not his balls. "But Monique is a woman, ma'am. Men aren't allowed to enter the ladies' dressing rooms."

"Well, if it will make you feel better, we can pretend you're a woman."

"What?"

"Sure! I can look at you like you're just my best girl-friend, helping me on a shopping spree!"

"But—"

Your voice seems to rise several pitches until it becomes the most intimate, teasing sort of coo—the kind of voice usually reserved for sharing secrets with other gals. "Aw, stop, now, Victoria! No ifs, ands, or buts about it, you get your pretty little behind in here, girl-friend, and help me decide what to buy!"

He is powerless to resist. Moving as if you were reeling him in by an invisible fishing line, he stumbles into your room, hips first. What he finds there is a quivering, sensual woman, more beautiful in her rich and immediate aliveness than any fantasy he'd had all day.

You are completely nude, as promised, and the soft curves of your body, the velvet texture of your skin, and the gentle scent of your femaleness—all vulnerable, and only inches from his fully clothed self—is more than he can bear. He doesn't dare touch you (he's at work, after all!), but even without the provocation of physical contact, he comes wildly inside his pants. He tries to hide his orgasm, but no matter how still he stands, you can see the twists of his tender face and hear the exhalation of breath he can't control. Sated, he sinks to the little shelf-seat that juts out from the dressing-room wall.

You act as if nothing happened, tossing it off with a light "shop till you drop" remark, but the spectacle of his clandestine climax brought about by nothing but your naked presence has made your own juices flow with abandon between your legs while a breathy excitement builds in your chest. Slowly, you begin to undo his tie and unbutton his shirt. "Vicky, honey, why don't you model these togs for me?"

He raises his face to yours. A combination of fear, gratitude, and renewed desire fills the dark pools of his eyes. His mouth hangs slack with amazement.

"Me?" he croaks.

"Sure, girlfriend, why not? I mean, I can't really get a perspective on the merchandise when I see *myself* in it—I'm too hung up about my own figure," you say as you slowly caress your hips and belly, lingering for a moment on your curly mount. "And you'd look so lovely in these things, don't you agree?"

Completely entranced, young Victor/Victoria begins to shed his entire outfit, never once taking his eyes off of you, his sensual "sister" and playful guide. Stripped naked his body reveals itself as Adonis-like. He is like a perfect sculpture of maleness, from his broad shoulders to his slim hips, and his skin would be like marble if it weren't for the light carpet of hair sprouting from his chest, legs, and genitals. His recently spent penis is still surprisingly large, even in its softened state, and the massive head glistens with the nectar of his ejaculation. There is nothing remotely feminine about this fellow. And oh, how sweet is the contrast when you cinch his muscle-bound waist into the frilly lace corset and pull the strings tight. You fasten the push-up bra around his chest, tweaking each flat nipple as you do, then force his muscular thighs into the French-cut mesh panties with their little red bow at the crotch.

"Look at you, Vicky, aren't you just the most glamorous girl in the world?" you implore, as you turn him to the mirror. The sight of himself decked out in such intimate bits of clothing makes him weak in the knees, and his youthful prick begins to harden again. The thick bulge of flesh poking itself out of the delicate lace panties fills you with a craving you can't contain. You kneel to kiss it, and it responds even more to the touch of your burning lips.

"Oh, Victoria, you are such an affectionate girl-friend. I love our little moments together like this, with no nasty men to ruin our private pleasures."

He presses his lace-clad hips, bulge and all, into your rapturous face. But you have other things in mind, and you push him gently away.

"Well, I *think* I love the look, Vicky, but there's something missing. . . ."

You remove a long, silk cord from around your hair and use it to tie a beautiful bow—right around the base of his penis!

"There. All wrapped up, like the prettiest package."

With the delightful pressure of the silk tourniquet, his twice-aroused dick is sure to stay hard for as long as you like, and you go to work finishing your masterpiece.

"I won't really get to see the whole effect until we've done something about those naked legs. Try on the garter belt and these sheer stockings. . . ."

This time he doesn't wait for your help. Eagerly, he snaps on the ladies' garter belt and turns it around to its proper position as if he'd been doing this all his life. Then he sits on the narrow seat and together you draw the smooth, black silk hose up his rough legs to the middle of his powerful thighs. With each "click" of the garter fastening onto the stocking top, his dick grows another inch. Now it's once again fully erect, no longer hidden in the dull recesses of his khaki pants but proudly displayed like a gorgeous accessory rising out of the sinful lingerie.

"My, what a beautiful model you are, Victoria.

Pretty as a picture. The only thing left to do is add a touch of lipstick. . . ."

You remove a dark red shade from your make-up case and stand over the seated figure of the sexy salesman in his delicate underthings. As you lean in to apply a thick "O" of red around his full lips, your naked breasts graze the puffed-out shape of his bra cups. You both feel your hearts skip a beat just as that strange and wonderful contact is made, and the next thing you know you are impaled upon his raging organ, riding bareback between his silk encased thighs, your hardened clit banging against the knot of the silken bow, as he transfers his lipstick to your own silently screaming mouth.

Nature Girl

Are you a free spirit? If so, you may not be interested in the artifice of complex courtships, social manipulations, or even calculated beauty rituals such as fussy hairdos and makeup. You are an earth mother, a nurturer—a lover of animals, sunsets, nature hikes, bare feet, and romantic-but-grounded men. And, incidentally, your effect on those men is dizzying. Most of them respond with an overwhelming erotic instinct to a woman whose sensuality is located not in a pair of high-heels, but in her unfettered spirit, her naturally free physicality, and her soul-felt worship of nature's divine rhythms.

*Y*ou are Mother Nature's splendid, graceful daughter—earthy, like the black fertile soil or the green aromatic blades of grass, but at the same time as ethereal as the dancing winds.

You wear nothing but pure cotton panties and a gentle flowing gown as sheer as a spider's web. Your hair is loose and free as it tickles your neck, back, shoulders, and breasts, and your eyes are as liquid and changeable as the sea.

Your secret pleasure is to wander through the play of light and shadow in the woods, filling the empty sky with ancient songs, and inhaling the rich, redolent scents of the glorious outdoors. On these sojourns into the deep you are free to grow animal-like and elemental, rolling with glee across a carpet of verdant moss, reclining with abandon on a padded bed of pine needles, answering birds with a sweet whistle from your wet, "O"-shaped lips, or crying like a beast in heat with a low and guttural growl from deep within your delicate throat.

You travel further and further into the forest's tangled mystery until you are quite sure there is no one who can spy you in this dark wonderland. Now, faced with none of civilization's propriety, it seems ridiculous to be clothed, even if only by a swath of gauze. With an audible "Whoop" of passion unleashed, you throw off your gown and toss it across a branch. Then, in an almost sacred striptease, you begin to wriggle out of your fairy-child panties in a slow, sensuous dance meant to seduce no one but the spirits of the grove. Softly humming an accompaniment to your private ballet, you shed the cotton garment like a sinuous snake shedding her worn-out skin.

If a spectator were to encounter you reveling in this forbidden place, he would drink in a vision of a fine-skinned nymph-maiden dappled in the light of the forest's clearing. He would find your lovely plump limbs and sculptural torso contorted in a ritualistic *tarantella* that unwittingly revealed a scandalous view of your charms. He would take in your *mons de Venus* sprung with a full coat of silky tendrils from belly to backside, as you unself-consciously gyrate your rounded belly to the beat of your dance. And he would fall victim to your angel face, unadorned by jewelry or makeup and as fresh as a streak of dawn, which rises up above your two breasts tipped by bean-hard nipples. But, fortunately, you believe yourself to be free of any intruder's prying eyes, and so you move without inhibition as you dance, and dance, and dance.

A thin film of perspiration begins to cover your

nakedness and makes your body's whole complexion glow. Your hair grows wild and curly, your eyes alight with passion's flame. You are working yourself into a frenzied agitation. As your spirit soars, your heart begins pumping furiously, inflaming all your extremities with a hot-blooded desire. The tiny nerve endings in your skin become sensitive and you yearn to be touched and stroked. The globes of your buttocks and your normally demure slit redden and swell, aching for attention. Your breasts, unbound by stays or brassieres, feel heavy and full as they fly about freely in your dance. Even your tongue is alive, stretching and curling out of your dripping mouth, searching for something—or someone—to satisfy its hunger.

Before you know it, your hands are traveling everywhere along your body, pinching, caressing, tickling, massaging. When they reach your swollen gash, they gather the hairs together and tug, pulling harder and harder, until they let go and the whole tuft springs back into place. Your fingers wind around the wiry tendrils, curling them into little corkscrew pricks and tucking them just inside your aching cleft. But your own intimate caresses can't quell your appetite, and finally, you wind your gypsy dance down to a slow waltz.

But now you are hyperaware of your tender, throbbing, enlivened body all exposed and vulnerable in its natural state, and you're enchanted by the way it contrasts with the intense, rough textures of your surroundings. How cruel the craggy bark on that fallen tree would feel against the precious skin of your inner thighs! Cruel and yet somehow right, you think, somehow necessary—doesn't natural law dictate that opposites attract?

You mount and straddle the felled maple and imagine yourself riding on a rugged, steaming stallion. Your pliant legs are forced awkwardly open by the massive size of this wooden horse and your netherlips are drawn far apart in this unguarded position. Rough nubs and turns in the hoary bark tease and punish the exquisitely tender membranes of your pink, slippery vagina—oh, it is too, too much!

Suddenly, your lewd reverie is broken by the sound of a footstep—not a paw padding or a hoof galloping, but the thud and crunch of a boot sole upon the twig-lined surface of the grove. You look up, crimson with shock and shame. Who is this man who stands in the clearing, partially obscured by the twilight's shadow? And how much of your bestial abandon has he witnessed? You jump off your mount, skinning your inner thigh in the process, and lunge for your curtain of clothing still strung from a branch. But in a heart's breath you hear his soft voice.

"Have no fear, magical nymph. I am only your true and humble lover. I have been standing here, drowning in the beauty of your dance. Now that you have discovered me, I am rescued."

He steps into a patch of golden light and you realize that he is, indeed, your true love, your soul mate. Like the dense and turgid forest, he is also a study in contrasts with your person—tall where you are diminutive, straight and narrow where you are pleasingly round, insistent where you are yielding, rough where you are smooth, dark where you are luminous. His face is covered in a tangled beard, but his piercing eyes are clear and uncluttered. Deep, limpid, wise and yet wondrous, they silently worship your being with their stare.

"Please, drop the unholy robe with which you hide your breathtaking splendor."

You let the gauze fall to your feet. It floats down in slow motion, taking with it any resistance or chill you might have acquired from this untimely encounter. Now your body is suffused with a warm flush, less violent than the heat of your dance, but more sensual and long-lasting; a slow burn rather than a burst of raging urges.

"Why, you've hurt yourself!" your lover cries. "Look, there is blood."

Alarmed, you look down to see a tiny, fiery-red

rivulet running from the surface wound on your thigh.

"It's nothing," you assure him, and begin to wipe away the almost insignificant line of blood. Before you can complete the gesture, he is running to your aid, dropping to the ground in order to heal the injury. He squats on one knee, in the pose of the chivalrous suitor, and braces himself by wrapping his arms around your legs and grasping your solid, full buttocks with his powerful hands. Then he softy, ever so softly, kisses the place where you are scraped. The salt of his lips against the abraded skin is piquant but not painful; rather, his sweet kisses and the movement of his light tongue, together with the tickling of his surprisingly silky beard, seem to heal any hurt and at the same time ignite your desires.

When he has tended to your tiny laceration he looks up at your moon-spirit face and searches for a sign. You smile and kneel to face him eye to eye. Without exchanging a word, you are kissing, sucking, your ripe mouth and tongue at last receiving the sustenance they've been craving.

Together, you slowly remove his clothing so that he, too, is stripped down to the essentials, a pure and lusty child of nature. As you embrace, you topple to the bed of moss and pine needles and roll about in a sort of languorous celebration. His rooting mouth finds your taut nipples and he begins to suckle like an infant, repeating between draughts, "Earth mother, giver of life, feed me your loveliness, feed me your soul."

His chant, his pressing need, his growing, throbbing penis searching for a port in the storm—all this makes you feel abundant and fertile, drawing your enormous store of erotic energy into one rushing wave, until you feel you are about to explode. His worshipful, hungry mouth sucking at your swollen breasts is like hot liquid ambrosia, and as a tiny drop of nectar forms at the tip of his erect organ, you feel another spray of wetness shoot from between your legs.

Now that you are lubricated, enlarged, totally aroused and enveloped in the hypnotic call of the wild, he enters you in an earthy, yet divine, coupling.

Stranger on a Train

Do you believe that "familiarity breeds contempt" in amore? But do you also agree that long-term commitment is the goal for a healthy and happy romantic life? Wondering how to reconcile this conflict? Simple: Conjure up wild, erotic adventures with the unknown Mystery Man of your fantasies, then hand the part over to your well-known and well-loved partner. You'll have the best of both worlds—all the excitement of anonymity and "danger," but with a man whom you can trust and who knows the moves that turn you on! It's a creative way to spice up "safe sex," so grab your trench coat and take a ticket on this runaway train of ecstasy. All aboard that's comin' aboard!

$\mathcal{A}$ strikingly beautiful woman traveling alone by rail knows better than to expose her alluring figure or deep-set eyes to the scrutiny of every stranger on the train. So for this night trip across the Continent, you cloak yourself in a baggy trench coat, wide-brimmed hat, and mysterious dark glasses. You think, "Keep to yourself, talk to no one, withdraw into your thoughts, your dreams, your fantasies."

Choosing a cozy little compartment, you settle down for the ride. First you dim the lights to a pale glow—dark enough to induce sleep, but bright enough to comfort you in this odd, semi-public setting. You remove your bra from beneath your clothing and slip it into your purse—ah, that's much more comfortable for dozing—and don a velvet sleep mask for when you're ready to blot out the protective night-light. But you're not quite ready to turn in yet, so you push the mask onto to your forehead, cuddle up on the velveteen window seat, and settle in for a bit of a read.

The train rumbles beneath you like a snoring beast. The rhythmic lurching of the car combined with the eerie light of the overhead bulb is hypnotic. Soon you lose interest in your book; it drops to your lap unnoticed and you find yourself staring mindlessly out the window at the darkened landscape—trees, meadows, telephone poles, a house, telephone poles, more trees, train tracks, fences, telephone poles, telephone poles, telephone poles. . . .

Your eyelids grow heavy, your jaw relaxes until your wet lips part, lying open and undefended, and you begin to sink into slumber. You muster enough energy to lower the sleep mask over your eyes, and then quickly start to float away. As you do, a warm sensual feeling spreads like honey through your legs, buttocks, womb, belly, and chest, and you shift subtly in the seat to better receive the sleep-inducing "personal" massage that the vibrating locomotive offers.

Time passes—without your notice—when suddenly you are shocked awake by a loud clap of thunder and a bright flash of lightning. As the sky unleashes a driving rain, the little light in your compartment flickers and then dies. You pull off your mask to discover that even the moon, so full and radiant earlier in the evening, is now obliterated by the ominous clouds of a raging storm. It is pitch-black in your compartment, but there's no need to panic—you can hear the muffled sounds of conductors comforting nearby passengers. You assume someone will soon reach your little cabin, with a calm, authoritative demeanor and reassuring words uttered in broken English:

"No prrroblem, no prrroblem, ees O.K., meess."

So when moments later you receive a firm knock on your door, you don't hesitate.

"Come in!"

A man, so cloaked by the darkness that you can't even see if he's wearing the official railway uniform or not, swiftly enters. Of course, you think, it must be a conductor—who else would come at this hour of the night and under these circumstances? But there are no comforting words; instead, he commands, "Put on the mask." His deep voice is electric. His elegant, unnamed accent only serves to up the wattage.

You should scream, run away, demand an explanation, but you feel yourself compelled by some unknown force to silently comply. You are completely overtaken with desire. Heart racing, you replace the velvet blindfold over your eyes, and the blackness around you deepens ten-fold under its snug fit. In this total darkness, all your other senses become exquisitely heightened. You hear the tiny, rough scratch of a match being lit as if it were a nuclear explosion, then sense the tremulous flicker of a flame. Even though you can't see anything, you are aware of the dappling light of a candle through the thick velvet mask, as it disorients your inner equilibrium in the most delightful way. You sink back into your seat and await further instructions.

But the stranger is a man of few words. Instead, he communicates his animal desires with touch—the caress of a thigh, an exhale of hot breath on the back of the neck, an earlobe nibble, a gentle bite. His large hands grope everywhere under the trench coat you had thought so impenetrable. Down inside your skirt, up under your blouse—he even kneels you backwards and peels off your shoes to work the tender, sensitive flesh of your naked feet with his hungry mouth. Blind, boundary-less, tumbling across the land in high-speed flight, the wet tongue and lips of one unknown man feel like those of a thousand as he kisses and sucks your toes. You lose all sense of where you end and he begins—you are he, he is you, you are everywhere. You feel hot, then cold, aching, then bathed in healing waters—all of it pushing you beyond the limits of your own body as the sensations come over you in rolling waves.

Finally sated with his feast, the mystery man kisses each tender instep good-bye, then begins to work his way up past your calves, your knees, your powder-soft inner thighs. Never fully undressing you, he makes his way across your body's terrain by gently lifting, draping, and rearranging your clothing just enough to allow his hands and lips to seek out your nakedness. He fondles, tastes, bites, and strokes your now liquid, burnished skin. But unlike the predictable American men you have known, this foreign *paramour* seems to work backwards. He starts first with your dripping pussy, probing and kneading with his thick, callused, unfamiliar fingers—ah, how that rude violation thrills—then travels smoothly up your torso to your unbound breasts. Working from inside and underneath your blouse, he unfastens the two top buttons and lifts out each of your breasts. This is the first time he has fully exposed any part of your body, making your trembling breasts available to both his touch and his vision. He steps back for a moment to admire their luscious, feminine beauty in the glow of the candle as they hang there, thrust up and forward by the half-buttoned shirt on which they sit, on display like rare *objects d'art*.

"*C'est magnifique,*" he whispers.

While still reveling in his voice, you feel him approach, candle in hand. There is a pause; you hold your breath. What is he doing? Suddenly you feel a sweet, warm flush on each of your nipples. Ah, oh God, my God, what is that? Mmmm, it feels queer and wicked and wonderful all at once, arousing your erotic ocean and focusing its whole surge into those tiny, erect tips.

Slowly, you begin to comprehend that the pause made by this nameless, faceless lover was for cooling a bit of the molten candle wax that he had dripped onto his own palm for a few seconds before pressing the soft, comfortably warm substance onto your nipples. Like a lascivious sculptor, he takes an impression of your secret, throbbing points for the sake of his art. He knew you'd gladly model your most intimate parts in exchange for the delicious, stimulating pleasure these waxen molds bring, as they gently squeeze and harden into snug mushroom caps on the tips of your up-thrust bosom.

In the strange nether world of your temporary blindness, a hundred years and a million miles might have passed, but it only takes a few moments before you feel the strong, confident hands of your mysterious traveling companion guide you to your feet and turn you around. You stand with your face pressed against the cool glass of the window pane.

He politely whispers, "May I, *Madame?*" (as if you could refuse!) and ceremoniously removes the oversized trench coat from your shoulders. He slips it on himself, leaving the buttons open and the sash untied so that the whole garment flows like a tarpaulin across his broad back and down to just below his knees.

He moves in close behind you. Enveloping you, he reaches around to lift your wax-anointed breasts so that they, too, are pressed firmly against the rain-spattered window while at the same time you feel the hard bulge of his penis graze your ass. Despite the combined protection of your skirt and his trousers, you can still discern the outline of his penis's elegant, blood-swollen head and feel the heat radiate from its seemingly endless shaft.

He unzips his fly, lifts the back of your skirt, and lowers the seat of your panties. As he slips inside you, your breathing grows heavy and gasping; it fills your ears, adding to the cacophony of the roar of the storm and the din of the speeding train. Sunk deep within your hot flesh, pressed up against your quivering buns, he finally allows you to remove the blindfold. You try to twist around to see the face of this dark angel, but he stops you with a whisper.

"Watch the rain. Watch the rain." You give up, embracing this secret experience with a total stranger with all of your body and soul. You focus on the crazy maelstrom outside as your lover lets the rhythmic lurching of the long, snaking locomotive ease his engorged dick slowly, steadily, in and out, in and out. . . .

Your shrieks of pleasure are drowned out by the mournful cry of the train whistle. Moments later, the conductor enters your cabin to announce the next station. All he sees is a happy couple standing together at the window, gazing contentedly at the passing countryside.

Romance Writer

Of all the fantasies, this one is probably closest to your real life. It doesn't involve mysterious strangers, outrageous costumes, or extreme behavior. What it does deal with is the universal need to keep the flame alive in long-term relationships. That's not always easy in this stressful work-a-day world, but with amour, anything is possible. So take heart (and pleasure) in this sexy vignette. And remember: Even if you're not a romance writer like our heroine, you're an endlessly creative being (all women are!) and your many talents deserve the nourishment and replenishment of a good, long, slow, sensual . . . you know what.

*Y*ou are a successful romance novelist, renowned for creating sweeping tales of love, lust, passion, and excitement. Every day you sit at your computer staring into the screen, searching your heart, soul, and imagination for just the right words to describe a character's gleaming eye or shapely bosom or the wave of desire that washes over her in a deafening swell. Hour after hour you invent mysterious, elegant, sensual lovers to sweep her off her feet, or rough, wild, forceful lovers to take her with unbridled passion.

The situations your fictional characters encounter are extraordinary and unexpected. Their lives take exciting twists and turns, full of romances new or re-kindled, and their deepest yearnings get satisfied in grand and often surprising ways. Yet your own life has become unbearably ordinary, even dull. While the blushing maids and *femme fatales* on your page make glorious, creative love with various dashing rakes, you and your husband haven't had sex in over a month!

It's not that you don't love each other anymore, or even that you don't find one another sexy, cute, or desirable. But he's a dedicated lawyer working on a big case and he's hardly ever home. Between his career and your book deadlines, rarely do you have time to connect, let alone ravage each other on a spontaneous, thunderstruck afternoon the way you once did (or the way Elena, heroine of your latest opus, *Splendid Secret*, does with her paramour Grant). Sadly, you accept the situation with a resigned sigh and try to focus your jaundiced eye back on the blinking computer screen.

You are almost finished with *Splendid Secret*, but the penultimate love scene isn't coming too easily. You go through the motions, typing out some semi-alluring ideas with a few fits and starts of suggestive dialogue, but you know it reads as false and mechanical. Eventually, you give up and just stare at the screen. This is it: the dreaded Writer's Block.

Suddenly, you remember a technique an old writing teacher told you about years ago—an exercise designed to break through this kind of thing. Instead of trying to drag yourself into your characters' lives when the ideas just won't come, she suggested you turn to a fresh page and start writing something entirely different, something personal about *you*. Closing your eyes, you take a deep breath and try to let go of all your self-censorship and critical judgment; slowly you begin letting the words channel through you, as though they come from the heavens beyond. What you get is an uncensored, uninhibited inner journal. . . .

Love, I love, I love you . . . oh, babe . . . hold

me . . . I want you. I want you, want, want want you . . .
I need . . . touch me . . . your kiss. I long for your kiss, your
soft, tender lips, your warm, wet tongue forcing its way into
my slackened mouth, opening my lips, reaming my lips, gen-
tly but firmly devouring me, devouring my lips . . . drink in
my soul, suck me, lick me with your probing tongue. Oh,
God, nibble at me . . . I want to feel you, slowly . . . take
your time, kiss, kiss my eyes, my cheeks, my neck—ah,
God!—my tender, blushing earlobes . . . ooh, that tickles!
. . . Yes, stroke me there, ever so softly . . . find now my nip-
ples, my belly . . . Oh, how I ache for your touch.

You wonder if this exercise will really help break the writer's block, but at this point, you don't care, you're breaking a sweat! In fact, simply typing these words, with your eyes closed and pictures of your handsome, sexy husband doing these things to you flooding your brain, makes you moist all over. Perhaps you *can* use some of this feeling to get back into the Elena and Grant scene.

You are about to return to your novel, but before you can hit the "switch-screen" command, you hear the low, resonant tones of a much more compelling suggestion.

"Don't stop."

You gasp. It's your husband! Home, in the middle of the day! You hadn't heard him come in, enter the room, and move silently behind you; you didn't realize that he was reading over your shoulder as you composed your embarrassing secret fantasy. You blush in places you've never blushed before.

"Honey! I was just—"

"Don't stop," he says again, his voice a seductive whisper that goes right to your groin.

Suddenly, he slips a blindfold over your eyes and you gasp again.

"What are you—?"

"Shhhh. Now let's see, what did that paragraph say?"

You can feel the electricity from his body as he leans in close, his cheek lightly brushing yours as he strains to read the computer screen in more detail. You feel his hot breath in your ear. You inhale his unique and stimulating aroma—a natural male perfume unlike that of any other man—and your nostrils flare and tingle. This signature aroma has always been a major turn-on for you, and you enjoy being marked with his scent that lingers for hours after you finish making love. It's like having an echo of his pheromones on your skin, in your hair, and in your intimate places long after the tryst is over. You softly sigh as you grow light-headed and woozy under the olfactory spell.

"Ah yes," he murmurs, reading, "*I long for your kiss,*

your soft, tender, lips, your warm, wet tongue. . . .' Well, wait no longer, my darling. I've been feeling a bit lonely myself, and I wish to oblige."

One by one, he does each of the things you've written in your stream-of-consciousness monologue, and you melt at every touch, kiss, and caress. But just as you are falling into the erotic abyss, he stops.

"No—" you cry.

"A moment, just a moment!" he reassures you with a kiss.

He crosses the room and pulls all the shades, and everything darkens. Then he lights a scented candle, and even though you are still masked, you can sense the moody, flickering glow which bathes the room in a romantic wash. The gentle scent from the little votive is enhanced by your thwarted vision, as is the sinuous saxophone coming from the CD player—on just loud enough for you to feel the notes sensually climbing up your spine, but not so loud that you can't hear each other's passionate groans.

In a heartbeat, he is back by your chair, gently guiding your hands to the keyboard.

"Write. Write exactly what you . . . like."

Blinded, barely able to breath without shuddering, heady and drunk with desire, you rely on your fingers to work without guidance because the rest of you is transported. As they spell out each new wish, your husband is miraculously ahead of the game; he seems to anticipate your every want and need before you even finish your sentences. Nothing is blocked here; in literary terms, this story of ecstasy is "writing itself."

He slowly strips you of all your clothes, exposing your perfect breasts, torso, arms, thighs, and buttocks to his amorous hands and lips. When you are entirely naked, he begins to tickle your private parts ever so lightly with a plumed feather held between his teeth. This is maddeningly arousing, and your hands absentmindedly drop from the keys as your whole body squirms wantonly in the chair.

But without stopping his worshipful feather dance, he nudges your hands back to the keyboard once again, whispering through clenched teeth, "Write . . . you're so talented."

"Mmmnn, no, *you're* the talented one," you chortle thickly, typing simply the word *"yessssss!"* and hitting the "copy" button over and over until the word scrolls forever down the screen.

When you are about to explode, he drops the feather and stands you up, naked and quivering before him. He binds your hands behind your back with a smooth, silken cord, ending any pretense about encouraging you to "work." Pouring a little scented massage oil in his palms, he rubs them together to warm up the precious unguent and then proceeds to rub you, head to toe, and back up again. This splendid massage awakens and arouses every nerve in your being, genital and otherwise. You feel as if your whole body is one giant, lubricated, shimmering sex organ.

"GOOD GOD-D-D-D," you cry, as you sink to your knees on the carpeted office floor. He catches you in his arms, cradling your throbbing nakedness in his embrace, and removes your blindfold.

There it is: your husband's beautiful, wonderful, familiar-yet-thrilling face, smiling down at you, beaming nothing but pure love and desire into your waiting eyes.

As he gently, slowly makes love to you on your office floor, you have just enough consciousness left for one brief thought:

"Elena and Grant have nothing on me."

Speed For this scenario of high-speed turn-ons and fuel-injected fun, crank up your CD player, oil down your leathery hide, and don your tightest little mini skirt—you're about to take the trip of a lifetime on the open road. Oh, and don't forget the proper driving footwear: stiletto heels! Come on, everyone has a secret pair of stiletto heels hidden somewhere in their closet, don't they? If not, feel free to paint your toe nails purple and accelerate barefoot. We know it's illegal, but now's your chance to push the limits, break those boring, sensible, safe rules. And anyway, you probably won't get away with it now that your mate has been made a Special Deputy of the Law—don't you just love a man in uniform?

". . . Gimme gimme gimme what you know I need, turbo charge my engine, baby, gimme spe-e-e-d!"

⁂

A Stradocaster thunderbolt rings out from the car stereo and is swallowed by the wind. Riding like this— fast, with the top down and the world flying past in a green velvet blur—nothing is reined in or pinned down. Not the music, not your tangle of thick, luxurious hair, not your wild soul. It's all free, tossed to the elements. Out here you are Goddess of the Road, and with the smooth leather head of the stick shift firmly in your grip, you abandon all nice-girl notions about following the rules or playing it safe. The hard stick shift rubs against your sensitive inner palm, arousing the nerve endings and simultaneously sending a flash down to your inner thighs. Then the sensation goes deeper, more pointed— an ache, a yearning, a warm insistent pulse in your briny lower lip. The wind whips at you like an angry master but you push back with a defiant chin and razor cheek- bones . . . violent strokes, cutting tiny, invisible lashes across the tender skin of your cheeks. Each microscopic cut leaves a delicious sting that emboldens you, makes you even more rebellious. The radio screams, *". . . this is the zone, baby, don't never slow down, I want spe-e-e-d!"*

Hey, why should the car be the only one with its top down? Wriggling, you hike up your tight little skirt, lift your legs, and pin your knees to the wheel in order to steer without hands. You maneuver your arms out of the straps of your tank top and pull it down to your waist, exposing your full, unbound breasts. All the while your knees are forced open and apart by the steering wheel and you feel a cold rush of air *whoosh* between your legs. Oh, forgot to put on panties . . . again. You curse yourself for being so damn easy, for giving up your charms without a struggle to the hungry, lapping tongue of the wind. But there's nothing you can do about it now— might as well let him have his fill. So you push open your legs just a little bit more and utter a low moan as the wind tickles, nibbles, and slaps to his heart's content.

As you bring your legs back down to the pedals and regain control of the wheel with your hands, your skirt remains pushed rudely up and you find yourself sitting bare-assed and all exposed on the leather seat. Delicate, tender, moist parts rub against the cracked and hardened rawhide. Doesn't that naughty mechanic ever oil this baby's interior? No problem. Reaching into the glove compartment, you retrieve a little bottle of scented massage oil. You lift one ass cheek and aim the bottle's nozzle toward the globe of flesh. You squeeze, and . . . ahh . . . a warm stream of oil shoots over your buns. You begin a sort of driver's-side "lap dance," shifting, bouncing and oozing about in the seat, rotating your hips and buttocks in time to the music, giving this baby the sweetest, smoothest "lube job" a hard driving piston machine has ever known. Your pussy lips are splayed open across the now warm and buttery leather of the bucket seat and your own "interior" starts to contract and release. Your newly liberated breasts, bouncing which each bulge and dip of the road, receive their share of love slaps and discipline from the ruthless wind. Your distended nipples tighten like a baby's fist.

As you yank the bulging stick shift into the next gear, you bear down on the gas, accelerating faster, louder, higher, to blast off! The wail of the next song starts up—screeching guitars and pounding drums. You throw your head back and wail along. 70, 75, 80 mph—in your chest there is a thick and pleasing pressure as you struggle to gulp in breath—85, 90—now you feel nothing but the delightful torture of the road playing rough with your tits and the beating pulse in your swollen clit—95, 100. *"Fr-e-e-e-e-dom, lemme hear it now."*

But what's that sound? It's barely audible over the heavy metal riff of the radio and the bellow of the wind, the shriek of the engine and your own bestial roar. But it's there; an egg-shaped moan—*whoo-ahh-oo*—a steady, insistent dissonance to your wild-child song. Shit, it's a cop. You consider the options: Outrun the bastard—there's no way he'll catch up to you in his laughable black and white jalopy. You are jungle-red and sleek, all sexed-up and ready to fly. He's loaded down with those flashing lights, that heavy iron meshing which turns his back seat into a leather cage for law-breaking little girls, and that aching, hungry siren wailing its complaint. Plus, how can he maneuver with that nasty nightstick hanging off his belt? Still, he is gaining on you. Well, you'll show him who has a nightstick of her own. You fondle your gear shaft and prepare for overdrive.

But before you can lay into the gas, you catch a glimpse of your pursuer in the rearview mirror. Square jaw. Broad shoulders. Full lips, but set in a thin determined grimace—this Studly Do-Right always gets his woman. Oh, and then there's *the uniform*. You'd forgotten about the uniform, both what it says—Law Man, the Big Boss, the Enforcer—and what it does to you: the thick leather belt and heavy silver buckle which lock away all those hidden treasures that a road warrior like yourself might simply *need* to liberate; the official badge pinned to his muscled chest—how you'd like to finger the hills and valleys of those letters-of-the-law. The power of the state rests upon this man's shoulders and threatens to overwhelm your rebel nature and make you weak in the knees. You imagine fondling the badge's contours as he simply stands there, silent and unmoving, erect and at attention, as he's trained to be, but all the while he's boiling. You see yourself licking beads of sweat off his upper lip, your wildcat tongue roughened by the sandpaper stubble of his beard. Then you would slowly, sensuously sink down his body, moving from his lips to his neck, easing past the button-down collar and tightly knotted official tie, until your pointed, probing tongue eagerly licks and tastes his badge's bitter metallic surface, sucking in its government-granted power. You think of the musky heat that would rise from the officer's blue oxford-cloth shirt and how the rough wool of his standard-issue jacket would rub against your vulnerable cheek. And all the while, you'd be fingering his nightstick, massaging it with the oil that slides over your ass. Perhaps just as you both begin to cave in and sink to your knees, you'd suddenly pound his badge into his chest, hard, so that he felt the violent stick of its pin. This would shock him into action, and you would have to be arrested. . . .

Another bent note from the siren wakes you from

this reverie. You are still poised to gun it, but instead of speeding up, you down shift. After all, would it really be fair to race a poor, defenseless policeman so "vehicularly challenged?" 90, 80, 75 mph—it's a shame, since your baby is built for high-octane trouble and feels hamstrung at such a poky pace, but still you ease up—70, 67, 60—and the wind grows softer and more like a caress than a slap. You *would* like to play "chicken" with him, if only he had an worthy set of wheels more souped-up and stripped down, like yours. . . .

Oh my god! "Stripped down?" What were you thinking!? As the police car pulls you over to a complete stop, you frantically attempt to wriggle back into your shirt. Hurry! The Law Enforcer lumbers up right next to your car (do they always stand so close?) just as you slip one arm through the right shirt strap. But the left side, the one closest to the upstanding Officer of the Law, still hangs languidly against your body. The thin fabric barely covers your engorged nipple and is held up only by the swell of your left breast; in order to keep it from falling off completely and exposing your high-beam headlight, you are forced to thrust your chest forward.

"May I see your license and registration, miss?"

"Whatever for, Officer? Did I do something wrong?"

"You were traveling way over the limit."

"Ah. Well, I really hate limits." You smile a petulant smile and shift in your seat so that the loose side of your tank top slides off your satin-skinned breast and reveals all of its fleshy curve and blinking, red nipple. "Oops."

"Okay, that's it. Speeding *and* indecent exposure. Step out of the car with your hands up."

As you swing your long legs out of the door and stand just a whisper away from your captor, your little skirt refuses to fall back down into place; now you are partially naked, top and bottom!

"Shall I keep my hands up?" you ask coyly.

"No, ma'am. Just put them behind . . . my head." You wrap your arms around his shoulders and place your hands on the back of his crew-cut head, pulling his face to yours. Tongue on tongue, reckless heaving—he presses against you and you feel his cold badge graze your exposed nipple.

Suddenly he pulls out a length of rope and gruffly binds your wrists together. You pull back in shock and stare into his grimly handsome face. Your dark eyes flash him a challenge. This rookie intends to rein you in, does he? You'll see about that . . . but he just smiles and murmurs, "Do the crime, do the time." So you throw your legs up and around his hips, lightly kicking him with the stems of your stiletto heels, and he carries you around to the front of your car.

During this little trip, you feel the smooth, round head of his nightstick working its way in and around your open pussy and ass—how could that giant shaft slip in so easily? Of course, it has been amply lubricated by the hot oil still dripping from your rotating pelvis. He deposits you face down on your roadster's hood which is still warm from the ride. Positioning your legs wide and splayed across the broad, red surface, he begins to frisk you.

"Come on, Officer Joe, see if you can teach this naughty little repeat offender how to be a model citizen; I dare you," you spit. But inside, you're thinking, "You keep this baby's engine all fired up, and she could learn to *love* the long arm of the law."

Best Boy

Popular theory has it that, when it comes to sexual turn-ons, men are more excited by visual stimulation than written, which is why so much of the erotica for men focuses on sexy photos rather than narratives like these designed to provoke the female imagination. But, like any theory, there are exceptions to the rule, and responses vary quite a bit among both men and women. So if you're a visual kind of gal who "likes to watch" (or be watched), this steamy scene might be just your thing! And if you've never considered the prospect of a little fantasy voyeurism, get ready to open your mind and your most intimate musings to all the lights, the cameras, and especially, the action. . . .

"*I* want you," the man whispers. He smiles impishly at the voluptuous blonde across the room, and although his command is barely audible, it causes her to stir. His broad shoulders and deep-set eyes are half hidden by an artistic shadow falling across his still figure; the bit of light that is available seems to quiver with anticipation. Slowly, his perfect lips begin to part and everything centers only on these moist, full cushions that open as he reaches forward, yearning to be fed. All else fades away as the couple cross the distance between them, enveloping each other in a deep sensual kiss. . . .

"Cut!"

The actors unlock their lips as a makeup girl rushes in to powder their brows and touch up *les bouches.*

"Was it me, J.P.?" the handsome-but-wooden mannequin with the star-quality lips calls out.

"No, Chad, you were good," you reply.

"Good?"

"Terrific. You totally hit your mark on that last kiss."

"Oh, then I suppose it was something I did or didn't do," spits the young starlet, She of the Talent-Free Zone.

"No, Sheena, sweetheart, you were fine."

"Fine?"

"Fantastic. Sexy, adorable . . . the whole *enchilada.* But we're having technical difficulties. I *hate* the light."

In a flash, the director of photography and the lighting designer pop up in front of your face.

"I'm sorry, J.P., I thought you said you wanted an artistic shadow to fall across him," the DP exclaims.

"Yes," you sigh, turning to the LD, "But does that tiny bit of light *have* to quiver?"

"Um . . . it's, uh . . . quivering with anticipation. Like it says in the script."

"It's quivering with a short in one of the electrical wires! Look, I am trying to make a movie here and I want to be able to see the damn thing! Fix it."

The two men skulk off to look for someone else to blame. You tell the rest of the cast and crew to "take five" and try to chill out with a bottle of Evian and a complimentary foot massage from that pretty little production assistant with the tempting cleavage and the luminous skin. You know she dreams of being just like you someday, and quite frankly, you find it a turn-on. You, who've spent your whole life wanting to make movies—not to be in them, like most star-struck American girls, but to *make* them, to express your own ideas and creativity. You suffered through the starving-artist phase but now you've made it—you are a *true* goddess of the silver screen. You can do it all, from epic love stories to high-stakes action adventures, from sensitive little "art" projects to blockbuster comedies. You are the one calling the shots, literally, as you are the internationally celebrated female film *auteur*. So why the hell can't you get a little thing like proper lighting on the set?

"Excuse me, Ms. J.P.?"

You look up, ready to dismiss whoever it is that dares to interrupt the kneading of your right metatarsal arch, but then you catch sight of a firm bicep being barely contained by the sleeve of a sweat-soaked T-shirt. A quick scan up and down this guy's body finds a pair of snug-fitting Levi's, a hefty pair of work boots, and a face like a dirty angel. Whoa. Tech guys are usually beer-bellied teamsters with bored expressions and a passion only for the doughnuts dispensed by the location cater-er, but this kid is different. This kid looks like he could be a Calvin Klein underwear ad.

"Who are you, young man?"

"Chuck. Chuck Conners. Your 'best boy'."

"I'll be the judge of that," you think to yourself. To him, you simply say, "Chuck."

"Yes ma'am. Chuck Conners. I just want to apolo-gize for the bad lighting. It was my fault, I shorted out a wire in one of the cables. I'm terribly sorry."

"Oh, great. My entire production grinds to a halt because of one dunderheaded techie! In case you hadn't noticed, I am *trying* to make a movie here!"

The kid doesn't flinch. "I noticed. In fact, I'm your biggest fan."

Okay, so maybe he's not a dunderhead.

"I've seen all your pictures and that's why I decided to go into film production," he continues. "Someday I want to make movies just like you do."

The ambitious little production assistant looks up from her foot work, a tiny worried wrinkle crossing her usually smooth countenance. You smile, enjoying the competition, and turn again to Chuck.

"Well, Chuck, if you want to make your own movies, the first thing you'll learn to learn is not to bust the nifty little lighting cables, okay?"

Then you offer up your other, currently unworshipped *pied* and dangle a bottle of massage oil in front of his breathtaking chest.

"And it couldn't hurt to get a foot in the door with the right people. Work your way in from the *ground up*, so to speak."

He regards your outstretched limb with a momentary sneer—he didn't approach the great lady of the screen in order to rub her feet!—but he decides to humor you. Clearing his throat, he hikes up his jeans, flexes his knuckles, and plants his heavy work boots firmly apart. Then he drops to a provocative squat right next to the industrious production assistant, and, displaying his bulging button-fly crotch front and center, goes to work on your soft pink toes.

The sight of the delicate redhead PA working next to this hunk of a best boy is immensely pleasing to you. You hold your hands up in the classic filmmaker's "framing" gesture to view the lovely composition. Then you get one of those rare inspirations for which great filmmakers wait a lifetime.

"Evan," you call to your assistant, "Break's over. I want everyone back to work, except . . . the actors." Evan looks at you with surprise. "Trust me. Release the bimbo and bimbette for the rest of the day, then get the crew back here ASAP. Oh, and get these two into hair and makeup," you add, gesturing to your foot masseuse and masseur. "We're about to make some movie magic. . . ."

"Okay, reset people. Places!"
"Quiet on the set, please."
"We have speed. . . ."
"And . . . action!"
"I want you . . . " Chuck whispers. He stands over a chair in the center of the set where your winsome PA sits

buck naked, hands tied behind her back and a mask over her eyes. Her breath is shallow and agitated and her pale, freckled complexion is flushed. You know the revealing blush is partly from the molten shame she feels at being so completely and mercilessly exposed to the leering eyes of the all-male crew, but you also know that the mask covering her eyes affords her enough of an illusion of privacy that she can also redden with lust.

Chuck turns directly to the camera, where your steady, watchful eye is fixed, and continues improvising dialogue, as per your directorial instructions.

"I want you," gesturing in your direction, "to appreciate the extraordinary personnel you've hired for this project." He sits on the padded arm of the chair and begins a slow, sensual tour of the girl's naked body, lightly touching, squeezing, and displaying each luscious portion of her intimate landscape.

"Her cinnamon hair . . . " he whispers, caressing her auburn tresses. "Her downy cheek . . . " his fingers graze her face.

Now his rough hands stroll down her neck past her shoulders until they reach her full, white breasts. Cupping one in his hand, he gently lifts it like a precious possession, an exotic object to be shown off to the camera's eye.

"Beautiful, Chuck, that's exactly right," you murmur, then you signal the DP to push in slowly for a close-up. You can feel both your mouth and your pussy begin to water as Chuck's face comes into the frame to suck and nibble your willing victim's tit.

Then his hot lips work their way down to her soft swell of belly, and as she moans, he deftly lifts her tiny round buttocks with one huge hand and holds open her swollen red cunt lips with the other.

You groan softly, now panting for the extreme close-up. But suddenly the dolly stops and you are no longer zeroing in on your lascivious subjects.

"What's wrong, Misha?" you hiss at your DP, but he doesn't answer. His dilated eyes have come out from behind the camera to stare more fully at the scene unfolding in front of it. Looking around, you realize that all the crew members are slack-jawed and trying to hide their arousal, as you too become aware of the beads of sweat dampening your upper lip.

"Guess I'll have to do it myself if I want to get anything done around here," you grumble. But secretly, you are pleased; the scene of the whole crew enthralled just adds to your own growing arousal. You take over the controls of the giant camera dolly, but just as you are about to reframe the shot there's more trouble on the set.

Chuck is still hunched over the wanton production

assistant who has now thrown her legs over the arms of the chair and is nearly unconscious with excitement. Her whole body is stretching and quaking like a skittish cat and she is right on the edge of coming as his eager tongue teases her aching clit into sweet oblivion. Then, all of a sudden, your diligent best boy up and quits his performance. Damned moody actors.

"Nope, this just isn't right," he sighs, completely breaking character.

The production assistant wails in frustration, poised as she is on the brink of completion. The denizen of camera men, gaffers, and script supervisors also weakly protest their own frustration with the *coitus interruptus*.

"What's the problem, Chuck? The scene was going great."

"Sorry, J.P., but I'm afraid I'm just not an actor." He brazenly crosses to where you are straddling the camera dolly's saddle (and surreptitiously rubbing yourself against the seat's pointy nub). He puts a hand on your shoulder and stares deep into your eyes.

"Like I said, I want to *direct* the movies, not appear in them. Same as you, Madame Directress," he adds, slipping his tongue, still soaked with his delectable co-star's juices, into your mouth.

"Oh, God," you moan. You should discipline the

upstart, but the tides are shifting, and you feel yourself becoming his thrall. The taste of that gorgeous young hussy mixed with the briny flavor of this talented stud is too much for you to resist.

"Okay," you whisper. "Direct me." He lifts you from the seat, slipping your panties off in the process. Then he carries you center stage, ousting the production assistant from her seat and depositing you there instead.

"I'm sorry, my dear," he tells the shocked PA, "but we're recasting."

He whips off her mask and her darting, wild eyes take in the room full of strange men who have been unable to control themselves after her recent performance, and who have fondled their penises into shameful release. The poor young beauty is flushed again and aghast; she bursts into tears and runs off the set. But you know she still aches for satisfaction, and from the corner of your eye, you see Misha slink off in her direction looking like he very much yearns to comfort her.

The camera is still rolling as the new *wunderkind* filmmaker frees his thick tool from his Levi's and guides it toward your open, waiting mouth.

"And . . . action!" he softly calls. Your elegant, experienced tongue goes to work.

"Good, that's real good," he moans. "Don't stop," he

directs, "I think we have a hit . . ."

But just before he comes, he pulls away from your wet and hungry maw. You are about to object, but he shoots you a look as if to say, "Don't forget—this is *my* movie!" and then swiftly crosses behind you, lifting your skirt to enter you doggie-style. He reaches around to place one gifted hand on your clit while the other cups one of your full breasts as it hangs invitingly forward. His fingers tug and play with your erect nipple as he begins to slowly, rhythmically thrust for your pleasure and the pleasure of all who have gathered round to focus on this naughty, lustful scene.

As the entire sound stage seems to explode in paroxysms of pleasure, and just before you pass out, you hear your young protégé yell, "*Cut!* It's a wrap!"

About the Author

Diana Riverside splits her time between New York City, Santa Barbara, California, and Paris, France, and is the author of numerous works of fiction and non-fiction. Ms. Riverside says the source for this foray into the genre of literary erotica is both her imagination as well as personal "hands-on" research in the field, making her a writer with a high degree of job satisfaction!